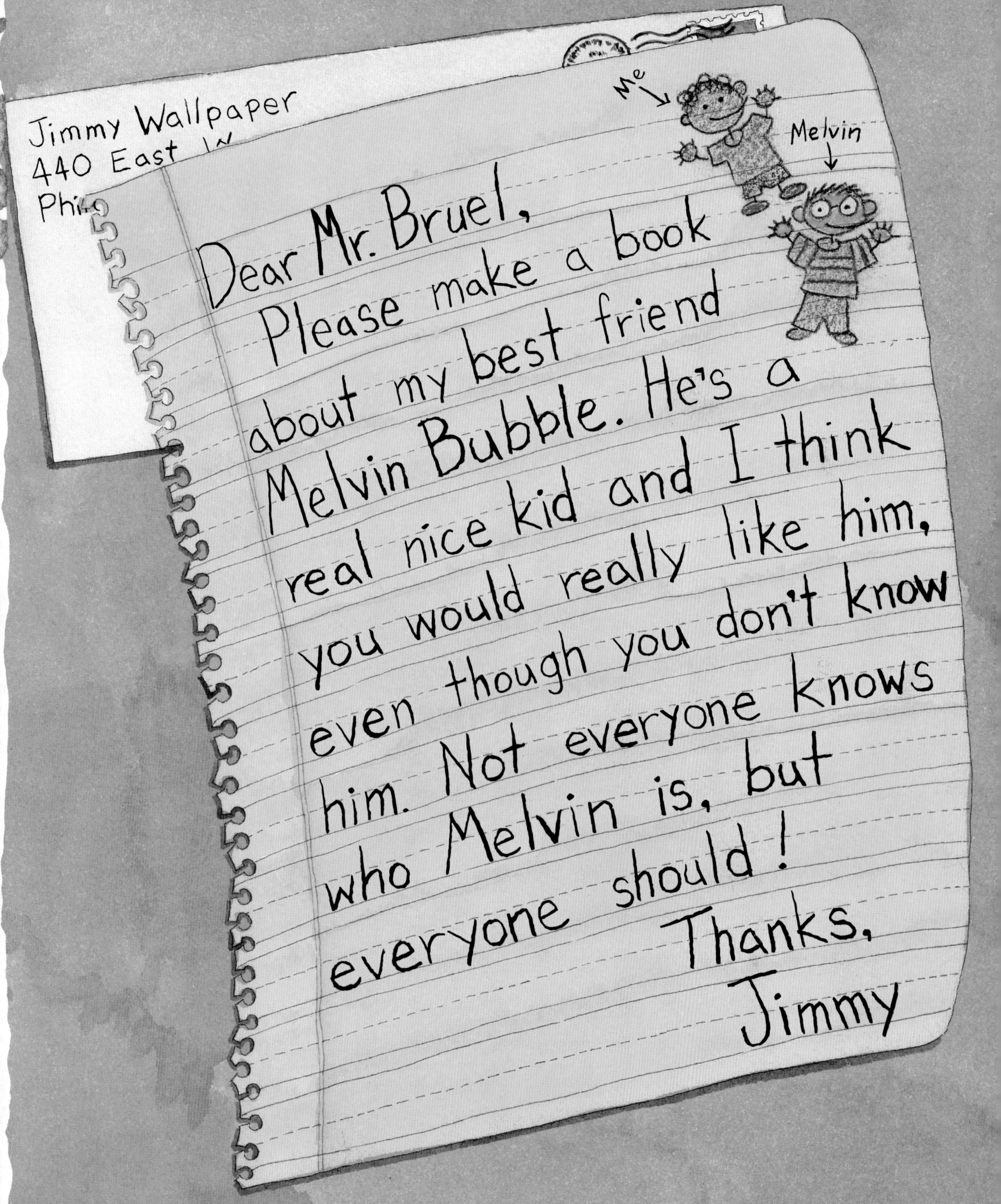

Jimmy Wallpaper
440 East W...
Phi...

Me →

Melvin ↓

Dear Mr. Bruel,
    Please make a book about my best friend Melvin Bubble. He's a real nice kid and I think you would really like him, even though you don't know him. Not everyone knows who Melvin is, but everyone should!
            Thanks,
            Jimmy

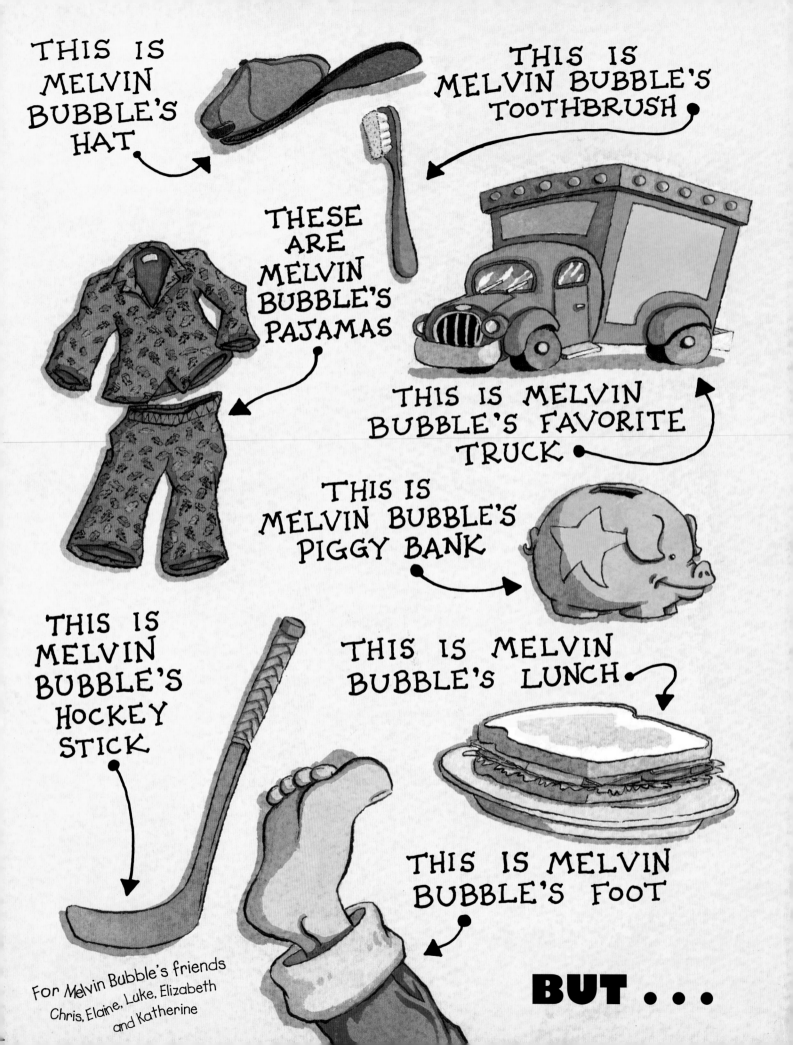

WHO IS MELVIN BUBBLE?

I AM.

By Nick Bruel

A NEAL PORTER BOOK
ROARING BROOK PRESS
NEW YORK

THIS

IS MELVIN BUBBLE.

BUT WHO IS MELVIN BUBBLE?

I DON'T KNOW. LET'S ASK . . .

Thank you, Sir. Now let's ask . . .

Do you see this? This is Melvin's sneaker! I found it under his bed in a box of crackers! I found his other sneaker on top of his lamp! I found his toothbrush in his sock drawer, and his socks on the dog! Once, I found his homework stuck to the wall with a piece of pizza! I love Melvin, but he may be the messiest boy in the world!

Thank you, Ma'am. Now let's ask . . .

So far, so good. Now let's ask . . .

. . . HIS DOG.

WOOF WOOF ARF WOOF WOOF BARK WOOF ARF BARK WOOF WOOF WOOF ARF BARK WOOF WOOF ARF WOOF WOOF ARF BARK ARF ARF WOOF

Good boy! Now let's ask . . .

GEE, I'VE KNOWN MELVIN FOR YEARS NOW! SOMETIMES, WHEN HE'S FEELING SCARED, I'LL GIVE HIM A GREAT BIG **HUG!** OR IF HE'S SAD, I LIKE TO GIVE HIM A GREAT BIG **HUG!** IF HE'S FEELING HAPPY, I'LL GIVE HIM A GREAT BIG **HUG!** ONCE, HE WAS REALLY ANGRY ABOUT SOMETHING, SO I GAVE HIM A GREAT BIG **HUG!** THAT MELVIN— HE REALLY LIKES **HUGS!**

MAKE SURE THAT'S IN THE BOOK!

Okay, I will. Now let's ask . . .

Hmm . . . Maybe we should move on.
Now, let's ask . . .

Thanks, Santa. Now let's ask . . .

I DON'T KNOW IF YOU'VE NOTICED, BUT THAT MELVIN— HE HAS A **BIG HEAD!** AND IT'S **HEAVY,** TOO! ONCE, WHILE I WAS DOING MY JOB, HE ROLLED OVER AND I WAS STUCK UNDER HIS PILLOW FOR THREE HOURS! I MISSED EIGHT APPOINTMENTS AND LOST MY HAT! BY THE WAY, HE SNORES.

**That's good to know.
Now let's ask . . .**

You may be thinking of someone else. Now let's ask . . .

WHAT KIND OF SILLY NAME IS THAT?! I HATE SILLY NAMES! THE ONLY THINGS I HATE MORE THAN SILLY NAMES ARE <u>PUPPIES</u> AND <u>RAINBOWS</u>! AND THE ONLY THING I HATE MORE THAN PUPPIES AND RAINBOWS ARE <u>BOOKS ABOUT PEOPLE WITH SILLY NAMES</u>!! MELVIN BUBBLE?! I HATE THAT NAME! AND IF HE WAS HERE RIGHT NOW, I'D KICK DIRT ON HIS SHOES! THAT'LL TEACH HIM TO HAVE A SILLY NAME!!

Okay! Okay! I'm sorry I asked! Yikes. Now let's ask . . .

. . . THIS MAGIC ROCK!!

Okay, so maybe it's not magic after all.

Now let's ask . . .

...A TALKING ZEBRA.

This is getting us nowhere, and we still don't know who Melvin Bubble is! Hey, I know! Now let's ask . . .

. . . MELVIN BUBBLE!

WHO ME? WELL...UM... MY NAME IS MELVIN BUBBLE. I'M 6½ YEARS OLD. I'M 4 FEET, 2½ INCHES TALL. I HAVE A **DOG** NAMED BUSTER AND A **TEDDY BEAR** NAMED CUDDLES. I LOVE MY **MOM**. AND I LOVE MY **DAD**. MY FAVORITE STORIES ARE **FAIRY TALES**, AND MY FAVORITE ANIMALS ARE **ZEBRAS**. MY FAVORITE HOLIDAY IS CHRISTMAS BECAUSE EVERY YEAR **SANTA** BRINGS ME THE BEST PRESENTS. I DON'T LIKE **MONSTERS**, AND I REALLY DON'T LIKE **MEAN PEOPLE**. LAST YEAR, THE **TOOTH FAIRY** GAVE ME FOUR DOLLARS AND THIS COOL RING I FOUND UNDER MY PILLOW!

AND MY BEST FRIEND IN THE WHOLE WORLD IS **JIMMY WALLPAPER!** I ONCE GAVE HIM A MAGIC ROCK I FOUND THAT GRANTS WISHES!

I WISHED THAT SOMEONE WOULD WRITE A BOOK ABOUT YOU!

Thanks, Melvin. Thanks, Jimmy.
See you around, guys.

Copyright © 2006 by Nick Bruel • A Neal Porter Book • Published by Roaring Brook Press • Roaring Brook Press is a division of Holtzbrinck Publishing Holdings Limited Partnership • 175 Fifth Avenue, New York, New York 10010 • All rights reserved • Distributed in Canada by H. B. Fenn and Company Ltd. • Library of Congress Cataloging-in-Publication Data • Bruel, Nick. Who is Melvin Bubble? / by Nick Bruel.— 1st ed. • p. cm. • "A Neal Porter book." Summary: An introduction to six-year-old Melvin Bubble as presented by his family, friends, and others. • ISBN-13: 978-1-59643-116-4 ISBN-10: 1-59643-116-4 • [1. Humorous stories.] I. Title. PZ7.B82832Wh 2006 • [E]—dc22 • 2005029551 Roaring Brook Press books are available for special promotions and premiums. • For details contact: Director of Special Markets, Holtzbrinck Publishers. First edition September 2006 • Printed in China • 2 4 6 8 10 9 7 5 3